Dog Tails

Adventures of
Three Dog Friends

written by Wendy Wax

illustrated by Michael Terry

Reader's Digest Children's Books®

Pleasantville, New York • Montréal, Québec • Bath, United Kingdom

"What a great day for a picnic," said Seymour Schnauzer, checking off items to go in his picnic basket. "Let's see…bagels, ribs, grapes, broccoli, and liver sandwiches. Now for the plan," he said. "First, I'll pick up Barney Basset Hound and Dash Dalmatian. Then we'll go to Bark Park. We'll play tag, then a game of fetch. Then we'll have lunch. But I better get going," he said, "if I want to stay on schedule. I sure hope that lazybones Barney is up by now," he said. "I better go see."

"Morning, Barney," Seymour said.

SNORE...SNORE....

"Come on, Barney," Seymour said. "We've got a busy day."

Snore...snore....

"WAKE UP, BARNEY!" Seymour shouted. "We're already late."
Barney opened one eye. "A late start is a great start," he
mumbled, then got a whiff of the food.

"I smell ribs. Is that breakfast?" he asked, opening the other eye in a flash.

"Breakfast is long passed. This is lunch," said Seymour. "And the quicker we get to Bark Park, the quicker you'll have some. Come on, let's go find Dash."

"There he is," said Barney, as Dash came barreling down the street. "Watch out, Seymour!" Barney yelled.

But he was too late. Dash was already jumping on Seymour, licking his face, and spilling the picnic basket all over.

"WILL YOU PLEASE STOP DOING THAT!" shouted Seymour.

"Ah, sorry. It's just I'm so happy to see you both," said Dash.

"That's great," answered Seymour, "but we've got a schedule to keep. Now help me pick up the food and let's get going."

"Okay," said Seymour, once they got to Bark Park. "Here is the plan...."

"Why do we always have to have a plan?" said Dash. "Why can't we just see what comes our way?"

"Like that train?" asked Barney.

"Exactly," said Dash, taking off after the train.

Before Seymour and Barney could blink, Dash made a
wild leap, and landed smack in the middle of the freight car.

"Hey!" shouted Seymour, "riding a train isn't part of the plan."

"You can't catch me. You can't catch me," Dash called over his shoulder.

"That's what you think," said Seymour, forgetting the plan and scrambling onto the train.

"Hey, fellas," said Barney, "wait for me." Barney tried to jump, but his legs were too short.

"Don't worry, Barney," said Dash, "we'll help you." And with that, Seymour and Dash pulled Barney onto the train. "Thanks," said Barney. "You guys are too fast for me."

"Okay," said Seymour. "Where were we?"

"Playing catch," said Dash, grabbing an old ball someone had left on the train.

"We play catch *after* lunch," Seymour insisted.

"Speaking of lunch," said Barney, "where's the picnic basket?"

"Oh no!" cried Seymour. "I left it at Bark Park. We've got to get off this train."

Just then, the train went over a bump, Dash dropped the ball, and *BOING*, it bounced on the ground. Dash jumped off in hot pursuit...then came Seymour...then Barney.

"Follow that ball," shouted Dash.

"No, Dash," yelled Seymour. "We have to get the lunch first." But Dash didn't listen.

If only we'd stuck with my plan, Seymour thought, as he took off after Dash.

"Wait for me," called Barney.

With all three dogs in pursuit, the ball bounced over a fence, across the grass, and into the river.

"Last one in is a rotten egg," shouted Dash, diving into the river.

"Swimming is *not* part of the plan," shouted Seymour, rolling his eyes. "But, oh, well, it *is* hot today," he said, as he dove in anyway.

"Not me," said Barney. "I can't swim. I'll just stay here and walk along the riverbank."

Meantime, Dash is still up to his tricks.

"Race you to the ball, Seymour," he yelled, and started swimming.

"But…a swimming race is *not*…." says Seymour. Before he could finish, Dash grabbed the ball.

"Here, catch!" he shouted, tossing the ball to Seymour, who caught it, and forgetting about the plan, threw it back.

While Seymour and Dash tossed the ball around, Barney wandered off. Soon he heard roaring water. He picked up his pace and followed the river. The noise kept getting louder, and louder, and soon he found out what it was. "Ohmygoodness," he shouted in one breath. "A waterfall! I've got to warn Seymour and Dash."

Off Barney went, as fast as his short legs could carry him, back to where his two friends were drifting—unaware— toward danger.

"Seymour! Dash! Watch out!" called Barney. "There's a waterfall up ahead!"

Immediately, Dash swam toward the riverbank. But the strong current dragged Seymour toward the waterfall.

"Dash, we have to help him!" yelled Barney.

"Hop on that rock, Seymour," Dash shouted to his friend. "I have an idea." Then he grabbed a long plank he saw by the water's edge. "Barney, when I put this across the water, you put all your weight on it. Okay?"

"You bet," said Barney.

Meantime, Seymour leapt from the rock to the plank, and walked safely to the river's edge.
"Hurray!" shouted Dash and Barney.

"Gosh, guys, thanks. You rescued me just in time,"
said Seymour.

"Even though it wasn't part of the plan," Barney and
Dash chimed in together.

"Thank Dash," said Barney. "He came up with a great idea super fast."

"Thank Barney," said Dash. "He ran like a greyhound to warn us."

"Well, you guys are great," said Seymour. "Even though it's scheduled for later...what do you say we eat?"

"Yeah," said Dash, "I'm hungry."

"Me, too," said Barney, "and I smell something delicious. Follow me."

Seymour and Dash followed Barney down a path and over a hill and ended up at a familiar gate.

"Hey, Barney, way to go," said Dash. "It's Bark Park."

"The picnic basket!" shouted Seymour. "It's just where I left it."

"All right!" said Dash.

"Good tracking, Barney," said Seymour.

"Okay, let's eat," said Seymour.
"I like that plan," said Dash, helping himself to a rib.
"Me, too," said Barney chomping on a liver sandwich.
"Hey, Seymour," Dash said, in between bites, "what's the next plan?"

"I have to check my schedule, Dash. But, hey, what about a trip to the beach?"

"Sounds like fun," said Dash.

"What do you think, Barney?" asked Seymour.

"Barney?"

SNORE. SNORE.

After lunch, the three friends walked home. Everyone agreed it had been a great day. Dash didn't realize it, but he was spilling the leftovers.

"Hey, Seymour," said Dash, "I'm hungry again. Was eating the leftovers when we got home on the schedule?"

Seymour turned and saw the empty basket.

"It was. But, well, let's forget the plan for once. Why don't you guys come to my house for some steak. Then the only plan for the rest of the day will be having fun."